Born to be Wild
Little Hippopotamuses

Colette Barbé-Julien

Words that appear in the glossary are printed in
boldface type the first time they occur in the text.

GARETH**STEVENS**

GS

PUBLISHING

A Member of the WRC Media Family of Companies

Staying Safe Next to Mom

A mother hippopotamus, or cow, gives birth to her baby either in **shallow** water or on the shore of a lake or river. A baby hippo, or calf, learns how to swim and walk a few minutes after it is born. It is too weak, however, to leave the water or the riverbank. The calf will

have to wait until it is about six months old to walk in the fields with its mother. Even then, it will stay close to her or another mother. The little hippo would be in danger if it is left alone. When it is one year old, a little hippo stops drinking its mother's milk and leaves her side.

A mother hippopotamus gives birth to one calf every two years. When it is born, a hippo already weighs between 65 and 110 pounds (30 and 50 kilograms). By the age of one, it will weigh up to 550 pounds (250 kg).

What do you think?

How does a mother hippo punish her baby when it **wanders** away from her?

a) She bumps it with her head.

b) She spanks it with her leg.

c) She screams loudly to scare it.

A mother hippo punishes her baby by bumping it with her head.

A mother hippopotamus weighs almost 4,000 pounds (1,815 kg) and is always ready to protect her baby against attackers. A hippopotamus calf learns that it must stay close to its mother, because hungry lions and crocodiles, and male hippos that often fight with each other, are dangerous. At the smallest sign of danger, a hippo calf quickly cuddles against its mother or climbs onto her back. If the little hippo moves too far from its mother's side, she bumps the calf with her head. And if it does not obey her, she bites her baby!

A young hippo stays close to its mother. The mother never loses sight of her baby and can always protect it.

On a quiet day,
a little hippo will
rest or play on its
mother's back.

During the first years
of their lives, hippos
are in the water more
than they are on land.
They can even drink
their mother's milk
underwater — without
breathing! When little
hippos are underwater,
they keep their nostrils
and their ears shut.

5

A Swim Before Dinner

Like their mothers, little hippos have very thin skin that dries out easily and cannot take the heat of the African Sun. To stay cool, hippos spend most of the day swimming in lakes and rivers. After the Sun sets, the hippos get out of the water to eat dinner. All the hippos go off to eat except for the littlest hippos that are only a few months old.

What do you think?

What do adult hippos eat?

a) fish from the rivers

b) giraffes from the plains

c) grass from the **savannas**

A hippo spends a lot of time in the water. Because its ears, eyes, and **nostrils** are all on the top of its head, a hippo can still hear, see, and smell when its body is completely covered with water.

Adult hippos eat grass from the savannas.

At night, small groups of hippos line up and walk to parts of the savanna that are as far as 2 miles (3 kilometers) away from the river. The savanna's grassy fields are where hippos eat dinner. For their huge size and weight, hippos eat only a small amount of grass each night. Because they stay motionless in the water or mud during most of the day, hippos do not use a lot of energy or need much food. When there is a **drought** and the grass dies, hippos can even go without food for several weeks. At these times, they live off the thick layer of fat beneath their skin.

Hippos do not use their teeth to bite off grass. They use their lips, which have a thick, hard skin.

Sometimes, when a mother hippo goes to eat, several young hippos that are not hers go with her. The smallest ones stay very close to her.

When hippo mothers go to eat, one mother stays behind to watch over the young hippos. She will protect all of them as if they were her own.

In the water, a hippo can float and move easily. It does not feel the weight of its heavy body. On land, hippos are still very **agile**. Even though they have short legs, they can climb up sloping riverbanks to reach the fields where they eat.

9

Every Hippo in Its Place

A little hippopotamus must learn the rules for getting along with other hippos. In the water, hippos all stand or swim in separate places. Young males and females that do not have calves stay together in one area. Mothers and babies

stand a short distance away. The mothers do not let male hippos come near their calves. The adult males gather around the adult females, instead, trying to get as close as possible to them. The males will even fight with each other to get the best places.

Hippo cows and their calves live apart from the large, dangerous males, or bulls. A cow watches over all her young: the newest baby, her two-year-old, and her four-year-old.

What do you think?

How does a male hippo show other males that he is in charge of a territory?

a) He ignores them.

b) He leads them to his favorite field to eat grass.

c) He sprays them with **dung**.

11

A male hippo shows other males that he is in charge by spraying them with dung.

The hippo bull in charge of a group of hippos will defend his territory. If another male comes close, he will often turn his back and spray the other animal with dung and **urine**. Male hippos also leave piles of dung on riverbanks and along paths to mark their territories. And all hippos use the water they swim in as their bathrooms!

An adult male hippo will open his mouth as wide as he can to show his power. Younger hippos then stay out of his way.

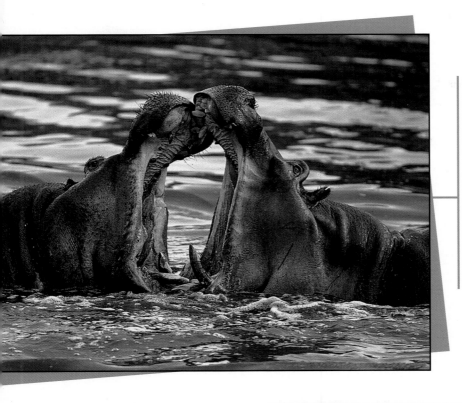

A male hippo uses his large teeth to force another adult male to back up and stay out of his territory. When the fight becomes more serious, their teeth can cause deadly injuries. A hippo's teeth are as sharp as knives.

The stronger of these two males will make the other hippo back up, and the winner of the fight will be able to stay closer to the female hippos. He will then be in a better position whenever a female is ready to **mate**.

Being Good Neighbors

Like their parents, little hippopotamuses go to the bathroom in the water. A hippo's waste helps the plants at the bottom of rivers and lakes grow better. These plants, in turn, provide shelter and food for fish. The fish attract birds — which eat the fish for their own dinners!

What do you think ?

How does a hippo get rid of the **algae** that grows on its skin?

a) It rolls in the mud.

b) It rolls in the dust.

c) It lets fish eat the algae.

Birds are helpful neighbors to hippopotamuses. The birds eat bugs that crawl on the hippos' bodies.

A hippo gets rid of the algae on its skin by letting fish eat it.

Because a hippo spends most of the day in the water, tiny plants called algae start growing on its skin. Fish help the hippo get rid of these plants by eating them. Except for animals, such as crocodiles, that might harm their young, hippos get along well with the other animals that live near them. They are afraid only of humans, who do not like to have hippos walking through their farm fields or tipping over and damaging boats traveling on the rivers.

Birds will stand on a hippo's body and use it as a lookout point. When the birds fly away, the hippo knows that danger is nearby.

Humans hunt hippos to sell or eat their meat and to sell their huge **ivory** teeth.

When they eat, hippos cut the grass of the savanna very short. They also squash some of the ground into mud. If there is a fire on the savanna, their actions will help stop the fire, so it does not spread from the grass to the trees.

The mud that hippos lie in helps keep their skin soft. It also helps get rid of insects and protects the hippos from insect bites.

17

Growing Up

Even though a young hippo grows larger, it continues to live with its mother for several years. A female hippo never leaves the group in which she is born. When she is about twelve years old, she will have her first baby. When a male hippo is about ten years old, he is considered an adult. Then he will compete with other males to prove he is better and stronger than all the rest. When a fight between male hippos takes place in the water, the loser leaves the water. When they are fighting on land, the loser lies down on the ground to show that he has lost.

Young male hippos imitate adult bulls by fighting. The young hippos fight with each other to find out which one of them is the strongest.

What do you think?

Why do hippos yawn?

a) to show they are tired

b) to show they are powerful

c) to show they are hungry

The leader in a group of hippos is the adult male that can throw back its head and open its mouth the widest. Young hippopotamuses do not dare open their mouths as wide as a hippo bull does. When male hippos become adults, they must leave their parents and the group of hippos they live with. When they are strong enough, they will fight to become leaders of new groups. The males that become leaders will have the right to mate with several females.

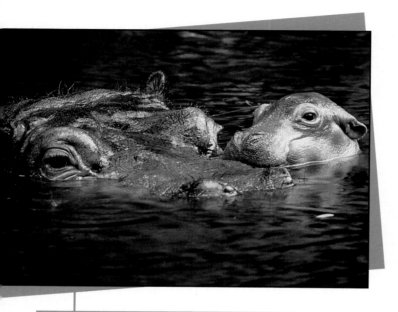

A female hippo usually gives birth to her baby during the rainy season, when there is plenty of water and grass.

The life of a young male hippo is not easy. Male hippos must be content to sit together in a mud hole, where they are barely able to move.

A hippopotamus's jaws have strong muscles
and bones that allow them to open very wide.

Hippopotamuses are **mammals**. They live in Africa, south of the Sahara Desert. Common or "river" hippos are found in rivers, lakes, and **wetlands** near grasslands. In the wild, a hippo lives from thirty to forty years. Male hippos can weigh up to 8,000 pounds (3,628 kg). Females are much smaller and weigh only about 3,000 pounds (1,360 kg).

Common hippopotamuses are related to pygmy hippopotamuses, which are very small and live alone, or with only one other pygmy hippo, in Africa's forests.

Although *hippopotamus* means "river horse," a hippo does not look like a horse. It has a big head and a long, rounded body on top of short legs.

Hippopotamuses are between 10 and 13 feet (3 and 4 meters) long and are about 60 inches (150 centimeters) high.

Hippos have thin, hairless skin that produces a red liquid that protects them from the Sun. A hippo's skin shows the scars from its many fights.

A hippo's eyes and nostrils stick out from its face. Along with the hippo's ears, they stay above the water when the hippo's body is underwater.

Male hippos have thicker necks than the females do.

Hippos can run more than 20 miles (32 km) an hour for short distances.

Although hippos have short legs, they move quickly on land.

A hippo has four **webbed** toes with hooflike toenails.

GLOSSARY

agile — able to move quickly and easily

algae — plants with no roots, stems, or leaves that live in water

drought — a period of little or no rain, when the land becomes very dry

dung — the solid waste of an animal; manure

ivory — the hard, yellow-white material that makes up the teeth and tusks of hippos and elephants

mammals — warm-blooded animals that have backbones, give birth to live babies, feed their young with milk from the mother's body, and have skin that is usually covered with hair or fur

mate — (v) to join together to produce young

nostrils — the outer openings of a nose

savannas — large, flat areas of grassland with scattered trees, found in warm parts of the world

shallow — not deep

urine — the liquid waste of an animal

wanders — drifts away or strays from a particular place or group

webbed — connected by skin or tissue

wetlands — areas of water-soaked land that are sometimes covered with shallow water

Please visit our web site at: www.garethstevens.com
For a free color catalog describing Gareth Stevens Publishing's list of high-quality books and multimedia programs, call 1-800-542-2595 (USA) or 1-800-387-3178 (Canada). Gareth Stevens Publishing's fax: (414) 332-3567.

Library of Congress Cataloging-in-Publication Data

Barbé-Julien, Colette.
 [Petit hippopotame. English]
 Little hippopotamuses / Colette Barbé-Julien. — North American ed.
  p. cm. — (Born to be wild)
 ISBN 0-8368-4736-9 (lib. bdg.)
 1. Hippopotamus—Infancy—Juvenile literature. I. Title. II. Series.
 QL737.U57B27 2005
 599.63'5139—dc22   2004065370

This North American edition first published in 2006 by
Gareth Stevens Publishing
A Member of the WRC Media Family of Companies
330 West Olive Street, Suite 100
Milwaukee, Wisconsin 53212 USA

First published in 2002 as *Le petit hippopotame* by Mango Jeunesse, an imprint of Editions Mango, Paris, France.
Picture Credits (t = top, b = bottom, l = left, r = right)
Bios: M. and C. Denis-Huot 9(r), 13(b), 15, 16, 17(bl), 22–23; M. Gunter 17(t), 17(br). Colibri: F. and J. L. Ziegler cover, title page, 22; J. M. Brunet 2, 3; C Ratier 7, 20(b); J. P. Paumard 8. Jacana: A. and M. Shap 4, 5(b), 12, 13(t), 18; S. Cordier back cover, 10; P. and J. Wegner 20(t); Mero 21. Phone: Ferrero/Labat 5(t), 9(bl), 11. Sunset: Horizon Vision 9(tl).

English translation: Muriel Castille
Gareth Stevens editor: Barbara Kiely Miller
Gareth Stevens art direction: Tammy West
Gareth Stevens designer: Jenni Gaylord

Printed in the United States of America

1 2 3 4 5 6 7 8 9 09 08 07 06 05